Emily Malbone Morgan

A Lady of the Olden Time

Emily Malbone Morgan

A Lady of the Olden Time

ISBN/EAN: 9783337113438

Printed in Europe, USA, Canada, Australia, Japan

Cover: Foto ©Andreas Hilbeck / pixelio.de

More available books at **www.hansebooks.com**

A

LADY OF THE OLDEN TIME

BY

EMILY MALBONE MORGAN,

AUTHOR OF

"A Poppy Garden," "Prior Rahere's Rose," etc.

"In her was youth, beauty, with humble aport,
Bounty, richess, and womanly feature,
God better wot, then my pen can report."

BELKNAP & WARFIELD,
HARTFORD, CONN.

To the Revered Memory

OF

LADY ALICE FENWICK,

WHO DIED AT SAYBROOK POINT, 1645,

AND

TO THE DEARER MEMORY

OF

ELIZABETH WEBB PRINCE,

WHO DIED JUNE 30, 1896.

☨

" Rejoice and be glad with her all ye that love her ;
Rejoice for joy with her, all ye that mourn for her."

" ON Saybrook's wave-washed height
  The English lady sleeps,
Lonely the tomb, but an angel of light
  The door of the sepulchre keeps.

" No roof — no leafy shade
  The vaulted glory mars,
She sleeps in peace, with the light on her bed
  Of a thousand kindly stars.

" She sleeps where oft she stood,
  Far from her native shore,
Wistfully watching the bark as it rode,
  To the home she should see no more.

. . . .

" By grateful love enshrined
  In memory's book heart-bound,
She sank to rest with the cool sea wind,
  And the river murmuring round.

" And ever this wave-washed shore,
  Shall be linked with her tomb and fame,
And blend with the wind and billowy roar,
  The music of her name."

Written by Miss Frances M. Caulkins of New London,
January 11, 1868.

Preface.

To MINGLE fiction with fact, to make character drawings of those who leave scanty records behind them, is like filling in the features of a beautiful or ugly face which is to leave as lasting an impression as any portrait or miniature. That such people lived, that they breathed, that they felt the weight at times, being human, of all this unintelligible world, history bears witness; while of the minds, the spirits, the material presence behind the outward act, even in the lives of more noted colonists she is silent.

Those, therefore, who would in a later age build their fictitious fabrics on slight foundations of historic fact, undertake a task which should be most reverently executed, for they deal with those who have passed into silence and can no longer speak for themselves.

The facts we have about Lady Fenwick herself could be easily compiled and stated in a very few pages. That she was tall and had golden hair we know. That she was religious is also evinced by her membership in Master Hooker's Church in Hartford. That she was a faithful wife and devoted mother we have also proof. Of her fondness for fruits and flowers, birds and animals, the meagre records also testify. That she was lonely and disheartened in this New World, yet bore up bravely, is implied. That longing for England she died and was buried at Saybrook, which she helped to colonize, is a matter of history.

I have tried to take these implied characteristics and develop them to their legitimate ends in the drawing of an ideal character. After some years' thought of her and study of these records I could not think of her otherwise than as beautiful and stately, a woman of strong mind and refined taste, of well-balanced judgment; a helpmate to her husband, a Madonna to her children, of most gracious presence and most winning ways. She was one of those transplanted flowers that blossomed in the springtime of our country. She could not for long bear the cold winters or the hard life of the Colonist, but in dying she left behind her a breath of the spring.

Records of such lives are like sweet pressed flowers, found in old family Bibles. Though the flower be dead the fragrance lingers. It penetrates other centuries, and breathes of something which in all ages has made life sweet and worth the living, bearing evermore constant testimony to the intense romance of History.   E. M. M.

HEARTSEASE, SAYBROOK POINT,
April, 1896.

Historic and Unhistoric Notes.

IN the following pages I have tried to be true to historic dates, and in order to do this have thought it wise to be guided by one historic record and that which I have been assured by the best authorities is the most accurate. I am therefore chiefly and deeply indebted to Dr. J. Hammond Trumbull's paper on the Fenwicks, which was prepared and read on the occasion of the re-interment of Lady Fenwick's remains at Saybrook in 1870. According to Dr. Trumbull, Governor Fenwick and his family landed at New Haven in July, 1639. Shortly after their arrival their daughter Elizabeth was born. Their younger daughter Dorothy was born November 4, 1645. Lady Fenwick died shortly after her birth in 1645. Mr. Fenwick returned almost at once to England still in 1645 or early in 1646. He received his title of Colonel while fighting in the north in the cause of the Parliament. He died in Berwick, England, in 1656.

In contemporaneous history the battles of Marston Moor and Cropredy Bridge, mention of which are made, both occurred in 1644, and that of Naseby in 1645. Herrick's "Hesperides,"

containing his poem "Divination by a Daffodil,"
was not published until 1648, in London, at the
Crown and Marygold in St. Paul's Churchyard.
Thirty years had elapsed since the death of his
master, Ben Jonson, and the poet was fifty-seven
years old.   During those years of troublous
times for England he had been quite free in
the circulation of his MS. poems, and it would
not have been impossible that some of them
found their way into Lady Alice's Commonplace Book.   Of the household of the Fenwicks
at Fort Point or Pasbeshauke or Saybrooke,
names all mentioned in Colonial history, the
ladies, Elizabeth and Mary Fenwick, are mentioned in the Winthrop Correspondence, also
Rev. John Higginson and Dr. Peters.   Of Peace
Apsley and Oliver Bouteler and Warwick, the
dog, no mention is made in Colonial annals.
That Lady Alice had a young cousin and that
her first husband, Sir John Bouteler, had a
nephew would not be strange, and that both
being young and comely, they should love each
other would be but fulfilling one of the most
natural laws of life.   The artist party who discovered Peace Aspley's diary had also an historic counterpart, and during one autumn made
many water color drawings from stenographic
views taken of the old fort and Lady Fenwick's
tomb, as it was before 1870.   There are other
interesting accounts of the Fenwicks and the
early settlement at Saybrook, notably in " Field's

Statistical Account of Middlesex County," " History of Middlesex County," " Hollister's History of Connecticut," "Connecticut Historical Collections " by Barber, " Dictionary of English National Biography " (Articles Fenwick), " Johnston's History of Connecticut," " Benjamin Trumbull's History of Connecticut," "A Gentleman of the Province," the book of Saybrook's Quadrimillenniel, and others.

A Lady of the Olden Time.

HE house nestled down by the water-side, surrounded by fruit trees. It had a low porch at the side that was covered with trumpet creeper, and there were marigolds growing in the dooryard. A grape arbor led from the old-fashioned door to the gate, and the artist inmates of the house called it the *loggia* among themselves, because it recalled the vine-covered terrace of the Cappucini at Amalfi, where some of them had once wintered. Outside the house had nothing to recommend it save that it was an unobtrusive brown foreground study against a lovely background of early autumn landscape, in those days when summer clings to all her sweetness most tenaciously and autumn begins to draw her veil of purple haze over hill and valley. Behind the house an old stone pier covered with the rank, brilliant, golden-rod, which grows in deepest yellow and orange only in the salt air, ran out some little distance into a peaceful cove, and beyond a quiet river flowed northward. At all hours of the day white sails glided lazily past the house and became lost in silvery distance. Across the river, church

2 (13)

towers rose white against the crimson-purple background of the hills, and beyond the cove the coarse marsh grasses were turning yellow, red, and brown, the concentration of autumn sun and shade, in the keen air of cool mornings and chill evenings. A road ran past the house and ended in a sudden curve, and a green field and some brown stubbly fields beyond hid the view of where the river met the sea. Across the cove to the west other church towers rose every evening, etched sharply against a primrose or violet sky. This was the late September setting of the plain brown house by the Connecticut roadway. Inside the house, life was simple, happy, and broad, for its temporary inhabitants were mostly citizens of the world, — seven cultured women, four of whom were artists, who were down there for an autumn holiday.

If what Marie de Medici once said is true, "that woman is always young, she is always twenty in some corner of her heart," they were all young; all at that age where aspiration stretches out her hand to Fame, believing sooner or later they will meet in a close handshake. Every day the artists made their way across the fields to the wharves, the lighthouse, and the sea, and returned at noon or night with quick and rapid sketches of passing ships, of weatherbeaten men mending fish nets in the sand, of the lighthouse against a brilliant cloud effect, or of a sunset over the marshes. They studied the sea in its every mood, calm, smiling, and indignant. Their sketch-books were full of sailors in every attitude and posture, and of the outline of trim, white yachts or ships with black hulks and weather-worn sails. Time was when the old harbor town with its present day picturesque lighthouse, breakwater, and wharves had seen much traffic. Ships that were not phantom ones had sailed slowly up the river from distant foreign ports, and the fort which once stood at the entrance of the harbor had figured largely in that which makes history. It was a great place for fisheries, and still within the memory of mortal man it was once equally a great place for clam chowders and Jamaica rum not always hidden under the rafters of old cellars. Salt tales of the sea were once in all men's mouths, and the place was full of the men who came back and had seen great sights all over the world, and of memories of the men who never came back at all. Old timbers and driftwood lying on the shore when the tide was low, the moaning pines over many ancient graves in the graveyard, rusting anchors half buried in the sand, all seem to tell the story that ever repeats itself, of a day that was past and of buried hopes.

Perhaps the inmates of the little brown house were more impressed with the inner history of the place than anything else, for the house itself had a history not wanting in tragedy or romance. Flavia, who was their hostess, and who had lived off and on in the house for many summers, had found out that it had figured in Colonial records. In their little parlor, which was littered with water-color drawings, sly caricatures, and sketches of each other, and more serious work on easels, as they sat round the fire waiting for the water to boil in the kettle on the crane for afternoon tea, and went to the corner cupboard for cups, they could not help wondering who had lived there in all those years since the Revolution, or who else had boiled water in the kettle and gone to the cupboard for tea-cups. They had been told when they first went there that an English officer had been killed in crossing the threshold, though some one else, who presumably was not present, was positive he had been shot in getting into the house · through the back window. That there had been much smuggling in those days there was little doubt. They had borrowed every book on Colonial history in the neighborhood, and spent much time in studying it evenings. They discovered that the modern method of smuggling was far less picturesque, at least that one ran less risk of being shot in trying to avoid official gaze in introducing into the country the latest styles of Madame Paris. At least, so thought Maud, their most special artist, a pupil of Dupre in Paris, a happy denizen for some years of the Quartier Latin, and thoroughly conversant with the small talk of the Parisian studios. She discovered a trap-door under her bureau, and said it led to some cavern of unutterable darkness, and it did, for it proved next day to lead to the coal-cellar. Somebody had taken occasion once during a dreary twilight, before the lamps were lighted, to tell them that some one had once fallen through that trap-door and never spoken again. Maud stuffed a comfortable under the bureau that night to prevent a sudden resurrection from the dead. Knowing they were intent on research, everybody kindly volunteered information, but as they voted not to be interested in anything that happened in this century, as it would be far too commonplace, the information did not always prove satisfactory. It left them, like hungry Olivers, crying for more.

One afternoon Flavia, who had been to the post-office, came in with a most exciting piece of news. Maud was toasting wafers at the parlor fire and Carlotta was passing around tea.

"Girls! What do you think?" she exclaimed, and then she went on to tell them how their neighbors not far off had only a few days before pulled down an old chimney, and found resting on the chimney-seat a pair of high-heeled white satin slippers.

"White!" said Penelope. "That sounds truthful. That chimney could never have re-

2*

quired a chimney-sweep!" But the others
talked her down, and Maud proposed pulling
down the dining-room chimney at once, to see
whether they also could find any.

Helen, the other special artist of the rival
school of Dupre, and who criticised Maud's
greens severely, was too absorbed in painting
a fishing scene in the corner to pay much atten-
tion, but Phillis, who kept house for them, was
quite appropriately excited, and Penelope, who
regarded all schools of art with patronizing
favor, and was longing for some excitement
besides the discussion of greens and ultramarine
blues, favored the pulling down of the chimney
at once. Adel lay back on the sofa and laughed
a low, musical laugh. Every household has a
center, and she was their center. Perhaps because she was always in one place, perhaps because a soothing kindness and brightness was
her atmosphere, and from her frail form seemed
to emanate a sympathy born of pain, because,
as she said, "she had always to go on all fours,"
as her faithful crutches bore witness; as Flavia
said, their household sun never went down, and
round her every lesser planet of the house
moved, as round the center of their being.
Carlotta, who sat at the tea-table, was her in-
separable companion. This was all of the
household in the plain brown house by the
Connecticut roadway : Maud, Helen, Penelope,
Flavia,—artists; Phillis, Adel, Carlotta,—home-

keepers, a very complicated art itself in the present day.

Adel's laugh provoked discussion. She apologized humbly, but said she did not believe in undermining old chimneys to find satin slippers of uncertain color.

"I have already forestalled any objections," said Flavia. "I have sent for a man to examine the chimney, and after the bricks are all pulled down it would be nice to turn it into a dear, old-fashioned fireplace, like that in Shakespeare's house at Stratford on Avon."

"Why not turn the house into an Ann Hatheway Cottage?" asked Maud. "I remember dining once at Charlecote Manor, not far away from Stratford, and being startled by my English hostess telling me that the house fairly 'stank of Shakspeare.' There, there, its a good, old English word, I know Carlotta is going to tell me, so I'll spare her the trouble."

"I was not looking in the dictionary," said Carlotta, looking up from a big book. "I was only rescuing our 'Historical Recollections' from an inundation from the tea cups."

"Carlotta has been poring over Colonial history all the afternoon," said Adel.

"What did you find out about this house?" called Flavia, taking off her hat in the hall.

"Not very much, except in 'Barber's Historical Recollections' I found a letter written from New London, and dated August 18, 1779, which tells us something about our officer who was shot getting into the back window."

"Read it," said Maud.

"We hear from Saybrook that a boat lately returning into the Connecticut River from Long Island, where she had been on an illicit trade, was stopped by the Fort at Saybrook, where a quantity of goods were taken out of the boat and lodged in the custody of one Mr. Tully, an officer of the fort, who stored them in his dwelling house." "This house!" interrupted Flavia, impressively. "On Sunday night, the 8th instant, eight men broke into the house with a view of carrying off the goods, on which the officer fired on them, killed two at the first shot and wounded another with a bayonet; on this, the others made off, carrying the wounded man with them. A warning to this kind of gentry."

"Dear me!" exclaimed Penelope; "it does not sound half as romantic as it did before."

"There is a map taken from President Stiles' Itinerary of Saybrook Point in 1793, which shows the position of our house and of other houses on the north cove!" exclaimed Flavia.

"How pleasant it would be to know more about the early settlement of the town," said Phillis, pensively.

"Carlotta and Adel ought to tell us something about it. They have been simply spending their time behind barricades of calf-skin books lately," said Helen. She had finished painting and joined the group about the fire.

"To most people," said Carlotta, "history, especially Colonial history, is not interesting unless sugar-coated and taken in homœopathic doses. To the earliest settlers coming here they found an almost unbroken forest. They found the oak, the pine, the walnut, the chestnut, the cedar, and the tulip tree. They found many wild animals and hungry wolves by the thousands. They found an abundance of wild fowl, turkeys, geese, duck, and great flocks of wild pigeons in the spring and autumn. They found, also, the red man, a wild people, who had their own wild religion and deities. In 1631 one of these red men visited the Governor of Massachusetts in the guise of a suppliant for his people. He described his country 'as of a fertile valley, divided by a river called the Connecticut.' He begged that both the Plymouth and Massachusetts Colonies would send men to make settlements in this valley. Governor Winslow of Plymouth consented to consider this plea. In 1633 men came from Plymouth and settled at Windsor. The Plymouth Company conveyed the whole territory, called the Colony of Connecticut, to the Earl of Warwick, which was confirmed to him by patent of Charles I. Robert of Warwick executed under his hand and seal the grant since known as the old patent of Connecticut, wherein he conveyed the same territory to Viscount Say and Seal, Lord Brooke, and others. Late in 1635 John

Winthrop, the younger, came to America as an agent of Viscount Say and Seal, with instructions to go at once to the mouth of the Connecticut and to begin the building of a fort, to be built upon a large scale, and to embrace within its enclosure ' houses suitable for the reception of men of quality.' The horrors of that first winter at the Point," exclaimed Carlotta, vaguely pointing out of the window as she spoke towards where the fort once stood, " were beyond expression. The cold was intense, the snow deep and drifting, and it was followed by the horrors of the Pequot War. Then came the first written Constitution, adopted in a general convention of settlers in 1639. And it was this same summer of 1639 that Lady Alice Fenwick arrived with her husband and other members of her household at Saybrook, for so the settlement was named, in honor of its original patentees. There had been a garrison kept up at the fort since its first erection by Mr. Winthrop in 1635, but no civil government was organized until the arrival of Colonel Fenwick. Among the first proprietors of this town were Captain John Mason, Thomas Tracy, Lyon Gardiner, who was the commander of the fort, and Thomas Leffingwell. The houses ordered had been built by Winthrop for gentlemen of quality in connection with the fort, so that Master Fenwick and Lady Alice, his wife, experienced less of hardship in carrying out their plans than was usual with the founding of new settlements. Saybrook at this time owed no allegiance to Connecticut. She had her own independent government, which was administered by Colonel Fenwick until the year 1644 or 1645, when it fell into the hands of Connecticut."

"Dear me!" exclaimed Penelope. "I never appreciated before that a little history went such a long ways, especially when there are no delicious court intrigues. I've heard all that old calfskin can give me in one day. Let's make our knowledge practical by spending the rest of the afternoon at Lady Fenwick's tomb!"

"Penelope!" exclaimed Maud, coming up to her and looking down into her face, "you are like all Americans before they have taken flight from the home nest, you would long since have gotten on your mental knees and stayed there before men who simply did their duty and struggled bravely against hardships, if you had lived in a country of Revolutions like France and saw what they did with their kings!"

Phillis ended Maud's rebuke by appearing at this moment with the clothes' basket. "If you are going to the graveyard," she remarked, "you might bring home a basket of pine cones for our twilight fires," and the family obediently disappeared to go in search of cones, leaving Carlotta poring over her old books lovingly; and Adel dreaming of the past.

Several days passed and the man whom Flavia had sent for to pull down the chimney did not appear. She waited till the fourth day and then started out with Phillis in pursuit of him. They walked for nearly two miles along a country roadside before reaching the town. It was the high carnival of the year for briars, brambles, and nettles, but they did not mind stopping to pick the odd, little stick-tights from their dresses, for the day was too beautiful not to study nature in her every mood. They noticed everything in that walk: the thistles blowing in the pastures, the meadows white with everlasting, just as everything around them was about to die, the milkweeds just bursting their pods with the wealth of white samite threads floating away on the September breeze, the gray green of the mullen spires against the fitful autumn sky, and the wayside tangles of Michaelmas daisies and golden-rod which they could not fail but gather as they passed. Phillis stopped, for her dress was caught in a blackberry bramble. Flavia tried to release her all in vain. And they laughed and talked and frightened a great flock of crows in the next field who rose with a Cassandra-like note in their "caw, caw," as they flew southward.

"They are singing the symphony of the dying year," said Phillis, as she gave a final wrench from her thorny captor.

"It always seems to me," said Flavia, "as if

autumn, like a gladiator, flung its dying salute to the world and going out in royal scarlet and purple set life to a triumphal march." "Do you seriously think we shall ever reach the town at this rate?" asked Phillis, and they hastened on to find that their delinquent man had already gone to pull down the chimney and that their walk had been fruitless. So they gathered great bunches of bayleaf and sweet fern, with a view to their future hearth fires, and hastened home to find all the dining-room furniture on the side piazza and a dust pervading the house equal to that of the tomb of the Capulets. The delinquent man had been loath to disturb a nice bricked-up chimney to find a possible pair of unmated, satin slippers, but the girls had been impervious to argument and so a heap of dust and bricks occupied the original site of the dining table and nothing was found as a result but a horrid dilapidated modern rubber shoe, which could not even be palmed off as a sandal of the early Greeks. The gentleman of the occasion carried a victorious smile on his countenance as he removed the bricks and mortar to the ash heap and went home and told his wife that there was not even an anatomical difference between girls and geese.

"It is a good-sized fireplace," said Flavia consolingly, but the girls were still very much disappointed about not finding high-heeled slippers and would not be consoled. They each took a hot biscuit from the kitchen table and went out to see the sunset, leaving Phillis to restore the dining-room to its original condition; and it was she, who, kneeling on the hearthstone of the new made fireplace and moving the bricks in the chimney, discovered poked far up on one side the little, old, discolored book, with its queer, broken clasp, which was far to outdo any mere high-heeled slipper interest and was to keep Flavia busy for many a day. When they came in to tea an hour later she exhibited her new-found treasure and they all examined it. It was closely written from cover to cover in a fine, and at times, indistinct, handwriting. Flavia examined it more closely after the lamp was lighted and found it to be some sort of a diary written at Saybrook long ago by one Peace Apsley, who signed herself a cousin of Lady Alice Fenwick, who had come with her to this new world and who had lived with her at the old fort. The writing was so fine and cramped that Flavia had great trouble in making it out.

"The spelling is so queer. It really needs to be translated into modern English to make any sense," she said.

"Let us postpone the reading of it until Saturday night when the house-uncles come down for their Sunday at the Annex," said Maud. "Meantime you edit it."

"Very well," said Flavia.

"To think it is our last week down here," said Phillis, sadly. "I wish the house-uncles could spend the whole week with us."

But the "house-uncles," which was the girls' name for their male relatives, consisting of brothers, cousins, and would-be sweethearts, did not appear till the late afternoon train, Saturday, as was their wont every week, putting up nominally at the "Annex," the hotel at the Point, but spending their Sundays at the little brown house. Flavia worked like a Trojan that week at Mistress Peace Apsley's diary to forestall the criticism of the house-uncles. There was Richard, Helen's cousin, and the would-be swain of Phillis, Mark, and Luke, anything but two evangelists, though called so derisively by Maud, and Harry, who belonged to the Society of Physical Research and was the most famous teller of ghost stories before driftwood fires on the American Continent. They arrived to find a supper of steamed clams and other fishlike productions that were eaten with a relish, and then, as it was a moonlight night, instead of gathering about the hearthstone, half the family disappeared in pairs into a moonlit world, so the MS. was not read until the next evening, which was chill and cloudy, and the warmth of the great open fire particularly grateful; then, seated in the chimney corner, Flavia read to them her translation of the diary of

Mistress Apsley, written at Saybrook in the years between 1639 and 1647.

♥♥

The Diary of Peace Apsley, of Apsley Farm, Surrey, England, written while in exile with her cousin, Lady Alice Fenwick, at Fort Point or Saybrooke, during the years between 1639 and 1647.

♥♥

I, Peace Apsley, spinster, write this record in exile to help me live through these weary days in a strange land. Outside I keep up a brave front, but inwardly my heart sinketh and when evening cometh and my dear lady and kinswoman no longer needeth my help and fellowship, I go and sit in the shady corner of the garden and look out over the sea and think of home among the Surrey downs and dream of the gardens I used to play in as a child. I can feel the breeze sweeping across the long grass of the meadows and hear the church bells ringing in the peaceful eventide, and see the rustic seat by the spring at the corner of the garden where my sister Rosell and I made cowslip balls each springtime. Ah me! shall I ever see or hear anything of them again? It was there at the beginning of the long meadow coming across the fields towards the stile where Rosell and I were standing, I first saw my Lady cousin's nephew, young Oliver Bouteler, walking towards us as the sun were going down. Shall I ever forget how he stopped a moment and looked across the stile at sister and me, as if he would fain speak, though prudence kept him silent, and then of how he turned in the curve of the meadow path and went away down the hill again as if he were walking away into the sunset, leaving us behind in dark shadow.

"A handsome youth," I said to Rosell timidly. "One seemingly well favored of God and man. I wonder whom he may be?" But Rosell said sternly, "Saw ye not he wore the King's colors and that he had too much scarlet in his doublet for a God-fearing man?"

Rosell were surely but a few years older than I, but forsooth she were born an aged maid and had not grown any younger since.

"Rosell, answer me this," I said, as we passed through the garden flaunting poppy heads. "Wherefor did God create such red heads as this if He wanted man alone to wear dun color till he put on his winding sheet?" But she were too pious to answer me. I hate God-fearing men with a whine in their voice. She can marry all the God-fearing dun-clad men she can find if it please her, though on thought a woman should be the wife of but one man at a time.

My eyes followed Master Oliver Bouteler as he walked away into the sunset and my heart all unknowing to myself followed my eyes after

3*

him down the meadow path, and when we went
into the house there stood our father greeting
him. He had come with a message of import
from our cousin, Lady Alice Bouteler, to tell
of her betrothal to one, a worthy gentleman,
Mr. George Fenwick of Brinkburn, Northumberland, a friend of my father; and of Master
Fenwick's recent visit to the new world colonies,
where my father had interests. Rosell had
gone into the house before me; I had lingered in
the garden and made a wreath of red poppies
for my head and fastened a great bunch of red
roses about my waist, to show my willful love of
bright color; so when I entered the great hall
after her, where Oliver stood, his back to the fireplace, I was indeed a maid abashed and felt like
Ophelia in the play. I gathered up my white
dress and would have run away, but my father
sternly called me, and I came back slowly.

"This is my daughter Peace," he said, "Master Oliver Bouteler. An idle maid with but a
fool's heart."

I looked up into Oliver's face. As he bent
low our eyes met, and then forsooth our hands,
while father frowned. He did not like me to
make so free, and scoided me well afterwards
and said:

"A maid with true modesty did courtesy to
the gentlemen, but kept her hands behind her
back."

All the evening I sat there quiet, my poppy

wreath and rose branch fading in the corner, while father praised Rosell as a good housewife, when Lisbeth, the maid, brought in the home-brewed ale and oaten cakes and Oliver unfolded the business which had brought him, not looking at me until the time came to say good night. Then he bent low once more over my hand, as if fain he would, cavalier fashion, press it to his lips, while I courtesied and he said low :

"Good night, Sweet Mistress Peace."

Ah! well a day! That were the beginning, but God only knoweth the end, as he knoweth the end of all heart aches.

After my father had lighted him to his chamber he came back and rebuked me sternly for my forwardness, and then said to Rosell in a stern voice that, though he were obliged to receive the message from his Lady Cousin and from his right good friend Master Fenwick, he loved not the messenger: that he belonged to an ungodly and God-defying generation, and had no fear of God in his heart, and was a defender of the King.

I am not very old, but, for an ignorant maid, have noted some things which I will note here, and one thing is that few men be God-fearing men or brave soldiers to those who fight in an opposite cause. I understand not these things, but think that it be a matter for which no man should be faulted that he stand by his King and his church.

Master Oliver Bouteler left at sunrise next
morning, after once more seeing my father. I
understood not fully at the time of the purport
of his visit. Those were the beginning of
troublous days for us and for England. Writing now in this lone spot, far away from home,
I can understand in part a little of what father
told us. Sometime before His Majesty, the
King, had dissolved his third Parliament, and
had granted a charter to establish a colony in
Massachusetts. My father's friend, John Winthrop, had sailed for Salem with a hundred men,
saying:

"I shall call that my country where I may
most glorify God and enjoy the presence of my
dearest friends." "Our hearts," he had said to
my father and others, "shall be fountains of
tears for your everlasting welfare, when we shall
be in our poor cottages in the wilderness."

He hath also written from the new colony
since:

"We now enjoy God and Jesus Christ, and is
that not enough? I never had more content of
mind."

Archbishop Laud of Canterbury, my father
saith, hath persecuted many godly men, Puri-
tan ministers, and doth encourage many Popish
ceremonies, so that thousands are seeking the
new world, where they may worship God as
they choose. My Lord Warwick hath bought a
fertile valley, called by some strange name, and

the Lord Say and Sele and Lord Brooke hath purchased a great tract of land by the mouth of a goodly river. My Lady Cousin's betrothed husband, Master George Fenwick, hath been sent out to the Colonies to visit it, and, in returning, hath reported that John Winthrop hath already dispatched a number of men to the river's mouth to take possession. A fort hath already been built under the command of a brave man, Lion Gardener, once in the service of the Prince of Orange, and houses are being built inside the palisades.

Master Fenwick, in his first visit to the new world, had greatly urged my father to go with him, but it were the summer before my mother died, and she were already ailing, and he would not leave her. Now Master Fenwick had returned, and he and my Lady had sent Oliver to apprise my father of their approaching marriage, and to urge that he would return with them to the new world, where he already owned lands.

This was the condition we were in, in England, when I first met Oliver Bouteler. Once more he visited us, to urge that my father journey to Teston in Kent, where my Lady still lived, near the estates of her former husband, Sir John Bouteler, and from whence she would shortly be married; that he would be present at her wedding, and that if perchance he could not come, Rosell and I be allowed to travel with old Lisbeth, under escort of her nephew, Oliver,

as she greatly desired the presence of her kins-
folk, — all the more that it were through her
cousin, Peter Apsley, of Apsley Farm, Thackham, she had first met Master George Fenwick.
How my heart failed me for fear father might
keep us at home, but, though he would not go
himself, having little love for weddings or gaiety
of any sort since my mother died, he bade Rosell
and myself make ready to accompany Oliver
under charge of old Lisbeth. He even called
me to him and gave me a brave white satin
bodice, with brocade petticoat of primrose silk,
with a brilliant for my throat, which had belonged to my mother in her youth; and Rosell
a gray satin, which had belonged to her later
years; and thus, well equipped, we started in
the early summer days for the wedding, escorted
by Master Oliver and old deaf Lisbeth.

What can I tell thee, dear diary, of that journey, of the meetings, and the handclasps, spite
of the vigilance of Lisbeth and watchful eye of
Rosell, who were fitted by nature to be a duen-
na by an extra eye, I verily believe, in the back
of her head. We said little, we looked much.
Each flower by the roadside, from the day's-eye
to the evening primrose, had its message, for
Love hath a language all its own, as the birds
have when they mate in the spring of the year.
We journeyed between green hedgerows and
summer forests, and rested one night at a comfortable inn, and then reached Teston and the

welcoming arms of the Lady Alice next day, — talking with our eyes of another wedding that might be when the next year were still young.

It maketh me unhappy to think or write of that marriage and how I danced till the early morn in my primrose petticoat, and of how before I left, Oliver and I plighted our troth in the dim old garden by the sun dial, which said on it : " *Post Nubila Phoebus.* After clouds a clear sun." Then we returned home once more, but this time Rosell took possession of Oliver and left me with old Lisbeth ; she would not let him speak to me, but would talk to him about the state of the times and of how the King were the ruin of England,— so we were not the merry party we were when we left Apsley Farm. The times and ourselves were out of joint. Rosell must have told my father something, for he treated Oliver with scant courtesy. So he abode one night with us and in the morning asked me of my father in marriage, like a right honorable gentleman, but my father answered him sternly that he would never marry his daughter to one who connived with popery, that he neither loved church nor state as it were then in England, and that he would sooner see me dead than wedded to a worshiper of Baal or the defenders of the devil's slave, for so he called the King. I heard it, for I was listening at the door, and my Oliver shamed me by his worshipful bow and said he would defer pressing his honorable

suit until the happier days which would soon
dawn. He left the house, but that evening sent
me a message by old Bardolph, the gardener, to
meet him at nine o'clock by the stile at the end
of the garden, near the long meadow where I
had first seen him, and then he told me all my
father had said and that he was going away and
that he could not tell when he would return.
Then we again plighted our troth together in
the moonlight, each vowing to be faithful to the
other until death should part us. It was solemn
as a marriage vow. He pressed a ring on my
finger and I gave him the riband from my hair.
He whispered every loving thing he could. I
kissed him and that was our farewell. I can
close my eyes and see it all now. I can feel
that last heart clasp. I can smell the roses as
they clambered over the wall and hear a little
bird in the thicket, who wakened at midnight to
sing a sobbing note at our farewell. The next
morning I went to my father and told him
everything, for there was nothing to conceal ;
but he was greatly angered at me and told me
" I were a pert maid without respect or modesty." He kept me closely in the house, only
letting me walk in the garden once a day, and
Rosell proved a good jailer. I have naught
against her. She were but an obedient child and
I a disobedient and rebellious one. In the
spring my cousin, the Lady Alice, was to sail
with her new husband for the colonies, and

coming to Thackham and seeing me pale and listless and hearing of the condition of things from my father, offered to take me with her, and I, longing to be with some one who knew and loved my Oliver, begged that he would let me leave home and seek my fortune with her in the new world. Thus we set sail from England the following April and after seven weeks, on the 20th of May, landed at Quillplack (New Haven) and from thence journeyed to this wilderness, where we have been for nearly four years past. I did not realize in leaving England I was leaving Oliver, until at sea my heart sank low within me. He was right beautiful my lover, tall, with a carriage of much dignity and of great strength, with hair of fine spun gold and a face such as he might have had who served King Arthur in the olden time and saw the vision of the Grail. He were merry and master of all manly sports was Oliver, and he now may be lying with his dead face turned up towards the sun, moon, and stars for aught I know, or may ever hear. I can write this now when the miles of lonely water roll between and no ship ever cometh from England to bring me word of him.

I have not yet writ at length of my lady cousin who is so good and kind to me, aye, and so brave, for oft I know her heart faileth her and she

4

longeth for the sight of home and kindred, yet
keepeth up a right good heart.   Oft as she sit-
teth at work I love to watch her, for she be
beautiful, tall and stately, with a head like a
Saxon princess, crowned by pale brown hair
that hath gleams of sunshine in it, that maketh
it seem at times like gold.   Yet it is not of that
outward beauty that perisheth that most becometh the Lady Alice, it is that quiet repose
and the spirit that shineth through her eyes that
seemeth to soothe all that is troublous about her.
I know not what my father may have told her
of my story.   I could but say to her briefly, " I
love your nephew Oliver."   And then I ran
away to drown myself in tears the day we left
England, and that is all that ever passed between us about my hopeless love, but sometimes
at even when I look perchance sadly and long-
ingly across the sea she hath come and stood
beside me and rested her hand for a moment on
my shoulder soothingly, and I have felt that her
thoughts had wandered back like mine to the
old home, her lost youth and her first love.
Then her eyes, with shadows in them like those
of coming tears, have met mine, and then she
has turned and glided away down the garden
path, her gray dress rustling against the prim
box border as she passed, and she has left me
feeling, though not a word has been said, that
she feeleth for me and knoweth that the wide
and cruel waters that roll between this new

world and home, divide forsooth my body from
my spirit, and that I left my heart behind me in
England when I sailed away. I can remember
when I was a child the first time I saw Lady
Alice. She had come back to Surrey with her
first lover and husband, Sir John Bouteler. She
was young and gay then, with a face as bright
as a fruit tree on a May morning. She were tall
and graceful, with a delightsome voice and
laugh. Not that in musing I would give a
thought that she be any way indifferent to her
present lord, Master Fenwick, he somewhat
grave and serious, having weighty matters resting upon his shoulders in the establishment of
a new colony. My lady cousin furthereth all
her lord's concerns with gravity and judgment,
only I knoweth she longeth many a time for
England, the home of her childhood, the scene
of her early married days.

When we first came into the wilderness we
suffered something of hardship, though Master
Chapman hath assured me that with a strong
fort and with many houses already built our
hardships were nothing to what they did under-
go who did first come here; how they could
not sleep of nights with the howling of hungry
wolves in winter, and for fear of the sudden
attack of the Red Man, who hath been quiet
since a bloody war that they had before
our coming, wherein much blood was shed.
But it seemeth to me still much hardship to

abide for long surrounded by savages and with wolves that howl so piteously in winter, though now we have a right goodly house and garden in the fort, and my lady hath lately united with Master Hooker's church in Hartford. The baby Elizabeth, who be named for our revered Aunt Elizabeth Apsley, hath been baptized. We be situated at the mouth of a beautiful river where it meeteth the sea, and for so short a period the Lord hath greatly blessed us in our undertakings. Our household here now consisteth chiefly of the Lady Alice and her husband and Mistress Elizabeth and Mrs. Mary Fenwick, with grave Master Higginson as chaplain, and the baby Elizabeth. There be also many gentlemen supporters of Master Fenwick, of which I have met a few, notably Master Robert Chapman, Captain John Mason, and Master Lion Gardiner, whom I especially favor, though he be no longer young. Master Higginson be recommended to us by the reverend gentleman who came with us from England, Master Henry Whitfield, who is now settled at Guilford, to whom my lady gave some of her best cows of the stock we brought over, when we parted from him after landing at Quillpack, July 15th, 1639.

Good Master Higginson returned yesterday from Hartford, bringing with him some garden seed that hath been much grown yonder, and a

healing herb for my lady's garden. Her flower
garden beareth, after some years' care, many
a dear flower of old England, of poppies
and roses and daffodils, while yonder on the
sunny slope on the south side of the fort is the
herb garden from which my lady maketh many
a soothing posset for the sick. Thither the
bees and butterflies resort all summer days, for
here grow mint, marjoram, anise, sweet basil,
catnip, lavender, coriander, and summer savory.
Surely this new world be right pleasant in
spring and summer. The sky here is bright
and clear, and they grow many strange flowers
such as I never saw before. In the woods at
springtime I have found sweet pink and white
blossoms, and along the borders of the marsh-
lands in August, where I have ventured with
Warwick, my lady's noble hound, for company,
I have found tall mallows with great blossoms,
pink as roses, while in autumn the fields be
yellow with strange branching, golden blossoms
and purple with daisies of Michaelmas, but never
a primrose or cowslip have I seen here. The
winters are hard and the wind it bloweth fiercely
and ofttimes snow lieth deep on the ground
from November to May, and we dare not venture forth but for a breath of fresh air, but sit
dolefully in the chimney corner, while logs are
piled high and the fire is the only thing to
brighten this cheerless world of snow. 'Tis in
these long days that my lady cousin shineth

4*

as the sun and brighteneth us all by telling
many a story of her youth or of the Surrey
countryside, or by singing hymns and songs.
Indeed, musick be to us all a great solace. My
lady brought with her from England a most
profane instrument, a lute of ungainlie height, at
which Master Higginson looketh doubtfully as if
it were an instrument of sin, and methinketh Mistresses Mary and Elizabeth Fenwick thinketh it
also contributeth to undue levity when we think
gravely of the destiny that awaiteth our immor-
tal souls. I confess to thee, my diary, my sinful
thought that the Devil should not have all the
good musick, for if so, to us who be young it
maketh Hell an attractive, not a gruesome
place. I love, like King David, the sound of
psaltery and harp, but like best of all the right
merry music to which he danced before the
Lord with a good heart. What if my father
should see this? He would think me given
over to the evil one, and I do fear me much
that my heart followeth too much after gaiety,
and that I would rather dance this very moment
than to say my prayers. How well it be, therefore, that my father be safe in England and
cannot read this wicked little book of mine,
wherewith I wile away the weary hours. My
lady is so sweet she offendeth no one, but singeth hymns and psalm tunes with good will,
while Master Higginson and the Mistresses be
by, but when we are alone she singeth the love

songs of her youth, and those which were of fashion in England when we left home. There be one I especially love, written by Sir Charles Smedley, which she singeth with great sweetness.

> " Hears not my Phillis how the birds,
>   Their feathered mates salute ?
> They tell their passion in their words,—
>   Must I alone be mute ?
> Phillis without frown or smile,
> Sat and knitted all the while."

My lady also brought with her a book of old madrigals and catch songs, together with graver poems. She hath copied many of a certain Robert Herrick, a gentleman and scholar, whom she had known in England, for she hath great taste and somewhat a gift herself at poetry, and many a weary afternoon hath she wiled away for me as we sat at needlework, with ballad and tale, and when the time seemeth heaviest she will talk to all of us of the promises of my Lord Northumberland and of the many others who were coming from England to settle at Saybrooke, so that when spring cometh we have been all of us on the lookout for coming ships. My father, when I left England, extolled to me so greatly the housewifely virtues of my dear lady that I thought not of her other gifts and charms, but indeed hers be of the right

kind of piety that saith little but doeth much.
Though her great Bible with its silver clasps be
always open on the window seat in her chamber,
wherefrom she doeth read daily on her knees,
she be not an apt quoter of Scripture. Then,
too, she hath a love for all living things, for
birds and beasts as well as fruit and flowers,
and knoweth with little study the name of each
and the season thereof. She hath tamed the
wild pigeons till they feed from her hand and
hath brought into gentle captivity for the little
Elizabeth a whole colony of rabbits, which alone
do give us much occupation. Yet with all these
gentle traits she be a brave lady with naught
but the fear of God in her heart, for she ofttimes
ventureth far into the wilderness with naught
but her good gun and faithful dog.

To-day I have picked some strange flowers
of lavender color under large, brown leaves
and my lady hath had some planted in the
garden. This day week we received some trees
as a gift from His Excellency, Governor Winthrop, and hath set them out about the house.
Master Fenwick hath written to His Excellency
thus wise :

"If we have anything that could pleasure you,
you should freely command us, as I am pretty
well stored with cherry and apple trees of the
apples you sent me last year, but the worms

hath in a manner destroyed them as they came up." This did I write with my own hand to His Excellency, Master Fenwick, dictating, for which I received in payment a great compliment, that my hand was as my face, sweet and well favored.

❦❦

Dear diary, thou hast been but a wavering companion written at long intervals these near four years past, but henceforth I will endeavor me for a time, at least, to keep a daily or weekly record of our life, for perchance if I should ever again see Oliver, he might like to know how we had passed these dreary days.

❦❦

May 1st, 1645.— May Day, and I did not rise at five to wash my face in honey dew in the meadows, as was our wont at home, so that we might carry a bright face the rest of the year. I thought it not worth while, as there was no one to be bright and gay for, but at ten o'clock there was great excitement among us because of the arrival of a messenger from Boston from His Excellency, Governor Winthrop, with important despatches for Master Fenwick, and letters and packets which had come in a ship to Boston several weeks before. How happy was I when my lady gave me a letter and a packet from my sister Rosell, after

Master Higginson had finished one of his long-winded morning prayers. I could hardly wait to open it till I reached my chamber, when I found that Rosell had sent me a blue figured dimity with a white kerchief and lutestring ribands to make it fine with; but forsooth who is there to dress for in this fort save perchance Master Higginson, who is of a faith too grave to care for the gauds of a maid! I be not in Boston, sister Rosell, or in Hartford, where me heareth at times there be some gaiety, and life be not all prayer meeting and sleep, but at a lonely fort in the wilderness at the end of a long river, always looking out to sea for some one to come from England, and before my eyes one face, and listening for one footfall. Such is the sad teaching of love to women that they look on one and he becometh their world! I care not for the dimity and the ribands, for I care not for the swains of this new world, though some there be that favor me. I care much for thy letter and even for the message from my father, who hath exiled me from all I love. Foolishness it be for me to write thus to thee, my book, nevertheless, will I copy my letter from Rosell, angry as it hath made me, for it came from England and it may be all I shall ever receive from there, and it might be lost perchance.

"Sweet Sister Peace:" she writes, "Long have I waited for a safe messenger to carry thee these trifles, that by them thou mayest bring the new world gallants to thy feet when thou goest to Boston. I can see thee in thy new gown with the ribands fluttering and the kerchief about thy neck, and the brilliant which our father gave thee sparkling at thy throat, dancing perchance in some country dance, as we used to dance at Apsley farm on winter nights; as you danced one night with the right worthy Master Ducksworth in the oak parlor, in the pink satin bodice and green petticoat. Dost remember? Ah me! The times be changed. Lonely it is in the oak parlor of afternoons with no sound of laughter from the garden, and our father be greatly puzzled at the state of the times. No one cometh here but Master Ducksworth, knowing that I be fearsome and low of heart. Great things have happened since thee left England. A great man, Oliver Cromwell, who hath our father's full confidence, and who be a worshipful friend of Master Ducksworth, hath risen in our cause to lead our down-trodden people. He had raised a regiment of strong, brave men, fighting in the cause of the parliament and they have gained for us the Battle of Marston Moor. Father be now away with them and the days pass heavily. The King is with his routed army at Oxford, and now I would tell thee something of thy Oliver. Tear him out of thy heart, for he be unworthy of a true maid's fancy. His father, who forsooth was changed

from plain William to Sir William by our weak
King in 1641 hath already fallen at Cropredy
Bridge last year.   Thine Oliver is now Sir
Oliver Bouteler, and with the King at Oxford, a
friend of Prince Ruperts and thy father's
enemy. Through such as these our country
has been brought nigh to ruin. Let not thy
heart follow after him any more than it
would after strange gods. This is the time to
tear from out thy heart all unruly affections, so
our father says, and to labor and pray right
hard for those who fight for the deliverance of
the people. He saith with Cromwell, 'God
make our enemies as stubble to our swords.' I
doubt not but thy lover still love thee well, but
love thou not him. We must follow this most
worshipful leader, Oliver Cromwell, and hate all
those who have brought this trouble upon us.
Think well of what I tell thee, and if some
serious and godly man of the new colony, such
as be Master Ducksworth, ask thee to share his
fortune, it would surely please our father much
if thou wouldest consent thereunto, for it would
give pledge that thou hadst forgotten thy old
and unworthy love, who followeth after Beelze-
bub and hath been led captive by the priests of
Baal. I send with this our most constant love
to our worthy cousin, the Lady Alice, and her
spouse.

« Thy Faithful Sister Rosell. »

To think I have laid waste so much paper to

copy this letter which maketh my heart to burn with anger. What care I for Cromwell and his cause? My heart is with Oliver, with the King at Oxford. My lover is a brave soldier. Rosell, what doth she know of love? a parrot writing but what our father saith, forsooth, and quoting to me Master Ducksworth. What's Master Ducksworth to me? Worth ducks and nothing more! Content myself with some man of this new world wilderness? It is well for her she can write of the trouble and stir in England for one who hath dwelt nearly four years one day like another and who would give all she hath for trouble and stir rather than to live through ceaseless days each like the other. Is not England a kingdom, and why should men not serve their king? Did I not promise to love Oliver, and do I not well to stand beside him? This also I know full well, if women had their way there should be no more war, but men should live at peace! The Lady Alice came into my room this even, looking pale and sad.

"Little Peace," she said sorrowfully, "there be strange news from home." I noted the way she said home and it brought dew to my eyes, for it voiced all that sad longing I had in my own heart. I handed her my letter from Rosell and she sat down in the window seat and read it. She smiled only once towards the end, and then looked grave again. My heart was hard.

"Rosell has never loved," she said, as she

5

laid it down. "I do not bid thee tear thy love
from out thy heart. I bid thee only turn it
upward; keep it still. It is God's sacred gift to
us. It must be trained, for it is human; it cannot be killed, because it is divine. Child, I have
known often that thy heart has gone outward
after thy lover; think of him less; think of thy
love for him more. He may never come back
to thee. Wilt thou repine? Wilt thou let it
grow bitter or wilt thou have it grow sweeter
each year a soothing posset for sick hearts?
Ah! nurse thy love. I tell it thee who have
also loved, yet loved not in vain. Let thy love
make thee brave for the whole, wide world,
Sweet Peace." Then she turned and I saw the
sunlight, as it seemed to follow her, as I lost
the sound of her light footfall on the stairs, and
my heart had grown soft as she spoke as if it
belonged unto a little child.

May 6, 1645. This morning I have been
taking down much instruction from my lady as
to the use of certain healing herbs, though for
many of these one might seek in vain at Fort
Point. There be herb two pence that be a cure
all, and the juice of buttercup doth stop sneez-
ing. St. Anthony's turnip be an excellent
emetic, and bindweed, pimpernel, and wood-
ruffe be cures also for blood and liver. I shall in
the leisure time of summer make pillows of
sweet thyme, mingled with poppy seed, which
be excellent to bring sleep to weary eyes, so
saith my lady.

There be talk at the present time of Master
Higginson soon leaving us to become assistant
of Rev. Henry Whitfield at Guilford, for which
I confide to thee alone, my diary, that I shall
not grieve if this be true. He be a righteous
young man, but I like not over righteous young
men, however grave they may be when they
be old and have wedded twice, perchance.
Master Higginson seemeth to have a liking for
me, and I doubt not that if I favored his suit
there might be a wedding at Fort Point before
he left for Guilford, but indeed this may not be
so, but beneath the fancy of a modest maid.

June 2, 1645. A great surprise hath come to
me, for to-day I hath received a letter which
came in a packet from Boston for Master Fenwick. It be written in a handwriting exceed-
ing precious to me and which maketh my
heart to beat quickly. Surely the times be
changing, as I told my lady, when last night I
saw the moon over my left shoulder. Soon,
perhaps, we shall hear of ships coming to har-
bour here or in Quilpack. My Lord Northumberland and the other patentees of the new
colony will come here and build goodlie houses
and plantations and my lady will no longer look
pensively across the sea and I can dance in my
sprigged dimity here without going to Boston.
But all this is not what I would write of, but of
my letter from my true love, that so thrilleth
my heart. This is what he hath written unto

me lonely and grieving at this Fort Point by
the sea:

"DEAREST HEART:— England and all the
world's at war because my Peace hath forsaken
her country and dwelleth among strange folk
across the sea. The light hath gone and must
somewhere be rising over the new world. I
wonder in these troubled days of civil war
whether thy heart still beateth true to one who
espouseth the royal cause and would die for his
King? If our cause seem lost and I can no
longer serve His Majesty I shall seek for Peace
over the water and verily not find it until we
are made one, for I am a Peace-loving man and
must be wed to Peace before my heart stop
wandering, 'chasing dim phantoms over path-
less seas,' as saith the poet. I wonder how and
where this letter may find thee. I have sent it
to one who is scribe to His Excellency, Governor Winthrop, hoping against hope that it
may sooner or later find thee. When shall I
look into thine eyes and feel I have found thee
beyond all peradventure? No man hath found
such Peace as I have found in thee, my be-
loved, or such large content as I shall have
when we meet again. Behold my heart hath
already gone half way across the sea to meet
thine, see that thine cross the other half to
meet mine, sweet Peace of the new world.

"Thine Oliver."

This be a verse or two of a right merry song penned by my friend, Sir Richard Fanshawe, for " the Saints' Encouragement " : —

  " Fight on, brave soldiers, for the cause ;
     Fear not the cavaliers ;
    Their threat'nings are as senseless, as
     Our jealousies and fears.
  'Tis you must perfect this great work,
    And all malignants slay ;
  You must bring back the King again
    The clean, contrary way.

  " The true religion we maintain,
    The Kingdom's peace and plenty ;
    The privilege of parliament,
     Not known to one of twenty ;
    The ancient, fundamental laws ;
     And teach men to obey
  Their lawful sovereign; and all these
    The clean, contrary way."

I know not what to think of Sir Richard's verse, save that it seem not respectful to either King or Parliament. It do make my head to ache to think which may be right or wrong, for verily there be good men on both sides. But war aside —

Did ever maid receive a greater reward for being true to her true love ? After long silence and loneliness and doubt if he be alive or dead, to have the silence broken by such sweet melody.

5*

I kissed the letter eighteen times this morning,
after reading it twenty-five, and then went out
into the garden to read it over in quiet. The
daffodils nodded over the garden borders, the
birds sang as if their throats would burst, the sea
looked bluer than ever it had done since I left
England, the sun shone as it never shone before,
and I wondered why my eyes had been blind to
so much beauty. I took up my lady's book of
love songs as I passed out, and after I had re-
read my letter and locked it safe up with drawings strings against my heart, I turned, for
greater comfort, to the book, and read some of
Master Shakspeare's sonnets and some written
verse of Master Herrick, copied full neatly in
my lady's own hand, and one written by another
was marked, and some one, forsooth, had written
a date against the lines, the date of Lady Alice's
first courting in breezy Surray, in the old Thackham gardens, writ one idle summer day:

> " There is a garden in her face
>   Where roses and white lilies grow,
>   A heavenly paradise is that place
>   Wherein all pleasant fruits do grow,
>   There cherries grow that none may buy,
>   Till cherry-ripe themselves do cry.

> " The cherries fairly do inclose,
>   Of orient pearl a double row,
>   Which, when her lovely laughter shows,
>   They look like rosebuds filled with snow.
>   Yet them no peer nor prince may buy,
>   Till cherry-ripe themselves do cry.

" Her eyes, like angels, watch them still,
 Her brows like bended bows do stand,
Threat'ning with piercing frowns to kill
 All that approach, with eye or hand,
These sacred cherries to come nigh,
 Till cherry-ripe themselves do cry."

" Reading love songs, Mistress Peace?" said a voice beside me, and I looked up like a frightened bird and half-hid my book, for grave Master Higginson stood behind the garden seat, looking down upon me with a searching look in his eyes.

" Yes," I answered, pettishly. Then he handed me, with a strange, new gallantry, four daffodils he had just plucked from the garden.

" Wear these as a nosegay, Mistress Peace; they well become thee. Thou lookest like April, as thou sittest there in the sunshine. Dost remember what Master Herrick writeth of the daffodil in Lady Fenwick's song book?"

" When a daffodil I see,
 Hanging down his head towards me,
Guess I may what I must be ;
 First, I shall decline my head ;
Secondly, I shall be dead ;
 Lastly, safely buriéd."

And he, too, forsooth, bent his head like the daffodil, low down a-toward me, looking into my eyes so close I felt his breath on my face, as if he fain would ask a question.

> " *First*, I shall decline my head;
>   Secondly, I shall be dead;
>   Lastly, safely buried.»

did I repeat after him as I arose. " Good
Master Higginson, I know you will rejoice with
me, for I have to-day received right goodlie
news from England, telling me of the health
and good faith of my one true love, who
fought like a brave soldier at Marston Moor,
and who, when last he wrote, was with the
King at Oxford. That is the reason, good
Master Higginson, thou findest me like a
picture of April, reading love songs by the garden wall.» And I left him standing there,
breathing heavily, looking far out to sea. Later,
in the twilight, when I passed through the garden, I beheld four daffodils lying dead on the
garden seat, waiting to be safely buried, and I
could not refrain from saying to myself:

> " First, I shall decline my head,
>   Secondly, I shall be dead,
>   Lastly, safely buried."

Oh! Master Higginson, grave Master Higginson,
surely thou thyself could have had but a passing fancy for one so gay, so trifling as this little
Piece.

June 16, 1645, Master Higginson talketh of
leaving us, and my heart is grave, for I fear me
much I may in some way be the cause. My
Lady looked somewhat sorrowfully this morn-

ing, when I came in from feeding the rabbits
and sat down to needlework. She had confer-
ence with her husband, and later she came unto
me and said :

"Thou hast caused sad unquiet and grief of
heart, Mistress Peace, to a good man. Master
Higginson be sore smitten of thee. Hast thou,
plighted to another, in no wise given him
cause?"

I could not bear that my lady cousin should
look at me thus gravely, but said that it were
surely a passing fancy of the good Master.
That even if my troth were not already plighted
I should make but a sorry show as the wife of
a godly minister, and my feet were going to a
roundelay in my head as I talked, till I looked
up and saw the Lady Alice's face filled full with
grave reproach.

"Talk not so lightly, Mistress Peace," she
said. "The greatest gift God giveth woman is
the gift of a good man's heart ; it may not be so
lightly spurned." And then I answered, with a
shake of my head and with spirit,

"Dear Lady, what can I do with two, but
keep the one already accepted and reject the
other. I cannot marry two." But I could bring
no smile to my lady's face. All she said in
answer was this :

"If Master Higginson remain with us, I beg
of thee to remember that by promise thou art
as wedded wife to another man, and there be

3*

others here whom I have noted thou treatest far
too lightly. I like not thy way of meeting
Master Huntington in the garden yester evening, nor thy free way with Master Baldwin when
thou didst greet him yester morn. Because we
dwell in a wilderness, dear cousin, there be no
excuse for forgetting we be gentle folk. I like
not to speak to thee thus, but thou hast com-
pelled me so to do." And she left me with a
very sore and angry heart, going like a windmill
in my breast. Surely I cannot wear weeds for
Oliver from morn till night. I be young and
the blood be not yet sluggish in my veins. I
like Master Huntington's glance of admiration
as I pass, and to have gay speech with Master
Baldwin, but I love none the less my Oliver. It
be all the fault of the godly minister, who hath
inclined his godly head and heart towards a
pert maid. So, dear diary, between ourselves I
consign these dog rhymes of mine to Master
Higgins, for forsooth I will not be courted by
any Higgin's son.

A dog rhyme written by Mistress Peace Apsley at Fort Point, June 16, 1645, and dedicated
to the right worshipful minister, John Higgins.

> Master Higgin's love lies bleeding,
>   While I pen this roundelay,
> I, relentless and unheeding,
>   Turn my face the other way.

Master Higgin's heart is broken,
  I won't mend the broken piece,
He to me no word has spoken,
  I won't come to his release.

For forsooth, it is immodest,
  For a maid unspoken to,
To wear her heart outside her bodice,
  Or bashful lover to pursue.

Master Higgin's sore offended,
  All because of little me,
Soonest gone is soonest mended,
  Better from the devil flee.

Cupid's dart or Satan's arrow
  Interfere with Gospel lore,
Stick in even saintly marrow,
  And there's always room for more.

" Daffodils for divination;"
  Master Higgin's are in vain,
Don't forget your ordination,
  In the mazes of Love Lane.

June 30, 1645.— I still be in something of disgrace, for Mistress Mary Fenwick looketh at me severely and my lady hath not sought my companionship of late. Can it be because of Master Higginson? How do the best of women exalt the godly minister and standeth him upon a polished stool and worship him above the common man, and wherefore should they, seeing

they be not uncommon, but of common clay, and
shall equally dissolve to dust like to ourselves?
I be not righteous, so I understand not these
things, but seeketh much the companionship of
Warwick, noble dog, and seek to know why
at times when one is sad of heart the brute
doth read the mind and mood and comforts by
silent sympathy — and preaches unending ser-
mons of deathless faithfulness from eyes lumi-
nous with love and gratitude, — when man faileth to understand. Talking to Warwick and
looking into his honest face I have renewed
my vows of deathless love to Oliver, for I would
be ashamed to be outdone by a brute in faithfulness.

Midsummer nearly, and my heart is very sad.
I be a most grave maid these days, quite far
apart from mirth, for time passes and no message cometh from England. Ah, well a day!
Master Higginson still be with us, more serious
than before and praying longer prayers. My
Lady Alice is not well. Let me whisper it to
thee, my diary, that in the autumn for comfort
during the long winter days God will send her a
blossom of springtime to nestle at her breast.

"God hath greatly blessed me," she said to
me yester eve, "for he hath sent me two children in this new world to comfort me for all I
have left in the old. My little Betty is a con-

stant joy, but she is fast forgetting her baby ways. Thee will find some day thyself, little Peace, that when a child nestles and lifts its little hands helplessly, then is a mother's fullest joy, for it is even yet as a part of ourselves and draweth its life from us as we draw our life from the Father of all. Poor men, they cannot understand this," she added low, as her husband came in with many papers of importance, to tell her of his appointment as one of the commissioners of the United Colonies at New Haven. He hath also received a letter from the court, desiring him "if occasion will permit him to go to England to endeavor the enlargement of the patent and to further other advantages for the country." There be talk of selling the Fort, as the gentlemen who thought of coming from England hath seemingly abandoned their purpose of emigration, and there be therefore little reason for our continuance here. I shall not soon forget the days of this long summer, when we have sat together working on little garments, or how calm and sweet my lady's face has grown in the thought of her little one and the white spirit that would join it at its birth. Once only has she voiced the light in her eyes; it was as she fashioned the little shirt to lie next the beating heart.

"Such gifts are a gift of the Holy Ghost," she said, "Sweet Peace." And a silence fell upon us that seemed to be none the less filled by the

6

stirring of wings. I love to record these thoughts of my lady in thee, my diary, because I want of her a picture for all my living days which will linger when perchance the vision of her comeliness and beauty be gone, as of a mind stored with all strong and goodly thoughts, as of a garden enclosed wherein grew all manner of fragrant flowers and refreshing fruit for way-farers. She seemeth in these days to have no longing for the olden-time and talketh but little of the past.

December 15, 1645.—A long, sad pause in thee, little diary, and it be a heart-broken maid that would record the days of our life at Fort Point since midsummer waned. Yet will it be some comfort, now that winter is upon us, to write of these days which have aged me and made me think like a sober maid. Through the summer we received no news from England. September came and the air became cool once more, for these new world summers be over warm. The great masses of woodland over the river grew hazy and purple, and at nights we sometimes saw strange lights of Indian fires. Great flocks of birds daily flew southward, and as we neared October the apple trees which Governor Winthrop sent us were, for the first time, heavily laden with red and yellow fruit. The days grew shorter and shorter, and after the sun had set the night became so cold that one could fancy that winter were no longer in hiding, though he wore a mask of yet warm sunshine by day. We were right busy in October preparing for winter, and my lady directed all things to be put in readiness for our comfort, and oversaw all that she ordered to be done. In the early days of November her little one came to her waiting arms, and was called Dorothy, because, my lady said, she was indeed the gift of God. She was a sunny little maid, and we needed much the sunshine, for after her coming winter set in grim and cold. I was always with the Lady Alice now, for she seemed to recover her health but slowly, though she were deeply happy watching the little face beside her, which seemed to be the summing up of her content. One night when I was sitting beside her she asked whether I had again heard from England and from him my heart loved best, and I showed her Oliver's letter, and she said it were the letter of a Christian man and one whom she herself loved.

"Be very true to him, Peace," she said, "and sooner or later thou shalt have thy heart's desire."

I would fain show by this how my lady felt toward Oliver, for there be some who would blame me for disobeying my father and clinging to one who were not of my belief, but though she were true to her own high thought

and followed after her husband in her desire
for freedom of worship, and condemned the
King, and believed that the days that were
coming to England under the leadership of the
great Cromwell, whom Master Fenwick had
known and seen much of in earlier days, were
better than those gone before, yet, forsooth, her
heart spoke louder for me than her head, and
she were ever one of those high-minded folk
who see good everywhere in friend or foe, and
dwelleth more on points of agreement than
those of difference.

I pressed her hand as I answered firmly, " I
will be true to Oliver Bouteler, thy nephew and
my affianced lord."

Then the little Dorothy cried, and we both
forgot ourselves in soothing her. That night
as I was braiding my lady's hair and rolling it
up beneath her white cap, she drew my face
down to hers and kissed me gravely and ten-
derly.

" Last year," she said, " when my husband
thought of returning to England I could scarce
contain myself for joy, but the year passed and
found us still at Saybrooke, and now I feel it
has been all for the best. Someone had to
leave home and come and make the desert
blossom as the rose; as well I as another. This
colony will grow, and mayhap some day those
who come after me may think gratefully of me.
Learn contentment here, as I have. I am

happy now, and no longer watch for ships far out at sea."

I know not why, or ever knew, why my father, after my mother's death, had me christened Peace, for I be of a most turbulent mind; but as I listened to the Lady Alice I became for a time quiet like my name. I left her with the baby Dorothy asleep on her arm, little thinking of the morrow or what the night might bring forth. It was towards midnight that Mistress Elizabeth came and roused me.

"Hasten!" she said, "if thou wouldst see thy cousin yet alive, for she is ill unto death."

I rose quickly and hastened to her bedside. A sudden change had come in the night, and her heart had failed her. When I reached her she could no longer speak. Master Fenwick held her in his arms, that she might breathe more easily, and the little Dorothy still rested beside her. Mistress Mary brought in little Elizabeth to bid her farewell, and she smiled graciously upon us. The passage home was short. An hour later her frail body was silent; her soul was in a fairer port. It was then I realized all the Lady Alice had been to me, and of how, by her gracious smile, rather than over-grave word, she had won my heart's devotion and guided my giddy fancies and wild hopes.

When I saw her in the morning her beautiful hair was smoothed back from her brow, her hands were folded across her breast, her sweet

6*

eyes were closed, they no longer watched for ships far out at sea. The little Elizabeth had laid a branch of red oak leaves at her feet, and her head rested peacefully on a pillow of the white everlasting flowers, gathered from the fields a few weeks before. She lay there in state like a queen, with a smile of unsurpassing joy on her face, while all in our little colony gathered about her to do her homage, and old Warwick guarded the door of the room where she lay. We laid her to rest on one of those mild days of sunshine which do make us think of summer, though winter be already here. We covered her grave with pine and oak branches, and came back through the desolate garden, trying to comfort our sad hearts with thought of her quiet assurance forever, leaving Master Fenwick still standing over the place where she lay, as if stunned with his own death blow. This hath all happened in this sad November of 1645.

🙥🙥

There be talk now of the return of Master Fenwick to England, and last night he sent for me and gave me my choice, either to return with him or remain, but he hath plainly stated unto me that he goeth to England to endeavor the enlargement of the patent, and that if he be unsuccessful he may never return. He gave me to the end of the week to think of it, but my choice hath been already made to remain beside the quiet grave yonder which containeth precious dust, which hath in it the germ of everlasting life. It hath also been decided to-day that the Mistresses Mary and Elizabeth Fenwick remain here with the two children, under charge of our new chaplain, Dr. Thomas Peters, who came to us this year, Master Higginson having gone to be with Rev. Master Whitfield at Guilford.

December 20th, 1645. Yesterday Master Fenwick left us, and hath left a sadly vacant spot behind. My heart almost failed me at the last that I went not with him. My heart hath lost all its spring these days, and is buried in my lady's grave. The Baby Dorothy hath grown into a winsome little maid, and be our great consolation. I hath no word from England, and I almost believe Oliver is dead. How do I regret my sins of insobriety when I longed for all men's praise. At times the last word my lady saith cometh to me with comfort: " Be very true to thy lover, Peace, and sooner or later thou shalt have thy heart's desire." But I cannot, nay, I can never say with her that I no longer watch for ships far out at sea. Spite of the dreariness the winter is passing quickly. The snow lieth heavily upon Lady Alice's grave, but yesterday there came a day that had a breath in it of the spring.

Since last writing the little Dorothy hath grown to look more like my lady, and much care of her hath set me dreaming as to what my own children will look like. There will be six of them I be fully determined, and I hath already named them in my heart, for indeed one be put to sore straits for amusement during these long evenings, and it is for my children and children's children I keep these records of their mother's and grandmother's life at lonely Fort Point. At this moment I stop and look into my tiny copper mirror and find myself not altogether old or ugly. My mirror, in fact, telleth me pleasant tales every time I look into it. I like my hair, and my face forsooth be not ill-favored. I shall be quite content if my six children, for whom I write this diary, look like me; especially do I hope the girls will have my mouth, which more than one swain hath told me be right kissable. Now more than ever am I feared at the thought that aught but myself behold these pages written for my six children, when for aught I see I may sign myself Peace Apsley, Spinster, to the day of my death. The hound Warwick hath moaned greatly since my lady hath gone, and yester even I found him lying by her grave. He watcheth by Dorothy when she sleepeth, as if he had been left in charge of her. Verily, next to a good home and those that make it, from grandam to babe, a good dog friend should be the most to be sought and valued.

And now, dear diary, I have come to that part of my story when I am slow to record, even for mine own eyes alone, what hath happened in these early spring gloamings when we can once more live in the free air. I fear much that this might fall into the hands of those who would think me over-credulous, yet I wish for my own and my children's sake to record it, for to me the memory of what I have seen is sweet and wholesome, not dreadful or gruesome. One evening nearly a month ago I were standing at my old place near the garden wall, in the early twilight. I could hear Elizabeth laughing as she were going to bed, and Mistress Mary's grave voice bidding her be quiet. The birds had not stopped singing their even-song, when I heard a sound behind me, though perhaps it were less a sound than a breeze of soft and fragrant air, a sense of a presence near me, and then I turned and held my breath, for I saw my lady, just as of old, coming down the garden path in her dress of gray, and the last light of evening rested on her head like a golden coronet. She seemed to be coming from the house and turned neither to the right nor left. A smile was on her face. Then she suddenly vanished and it seemed only natural that she should have been there visiting her children before they went to sleep. I did not think of it as a coming back from the dead. Every night for three weeks I sat there at the same time,

watching for her coming, and each night she
appeared, then slowly vanished over the water;
but one night she turned towards me and I
felt her presence coming nearer and nearer, and
I smelt something like the odor of violets in the
spring. Something soft seemed to touch me, and
I felt restful and sure that the future would
bring a blessing, and that after waiting I should
gain my heart's desire, more than any day since
she went away. Next morning I had been out
with Baby Dorothy to feed the rabbits, and the
little white things were running all about my
feet, glad as we were to be in the sunshine. I
had fed my lady's birds and all the little living
things she had loved and cared for. I had
weeded the flower border and tended the herb
garden, when I heard Warwick give the deep,
baying bark with which he always greeted
strangers, but forsooth I thought not much of
it, for I had heard Dr. Peters say to Mistress
Mary that he expected Master Robert Chapman
to see him that day on matters of business and
dispatches recently received from New Haven.
But when later Mistress Mary called, bidding
me come in and tidy my hair, for there be some
one awaiting to see me, my heart beat wildly until
I stood in the living-room, and there he stood,
my lover, tall and unharmed, and twice as
bonny as when I last saw him, though somewhat graver withal; and neither Mistresses Elizabeth nor Mary being present, but just we two

alone at last, I did what a maid's heart hath prompted her to do in all ages when she seeth her lover returned from the wars,—flung my arms around his strong neck and buried my face on his shoulder, and asked him a hundred questions and called him a thousand loving names, and knew not whether my name were Peace or Mehitable, or whether the war was over or whether my mirror lied, but did know that it were peace for me all over the earth at last, and so he said also that Peace was declared for him, as soon as I allowed him breath to speak.

Of all we said and of all we thought and of all we planned that day, the 4th of May, 1646, not even diaries may tell. It seemeth a year, though it be but a few days ago. Those who have waited and watched and grown heart-sick and then have had it cease will know, and to those who have not it would be hardly worth the telling.

That evening Oliver told us all that had happened in England during the past year. He had left home, being no longer of use to his King, and in answer to a message from Master Fenwick, through my lady's good word for us, bidding him seek me at Fort Point, and for her dear sake he had given him letters to His Excellency, Governor Winthrop, and others

high in authority, that he coming almost as
a fugitive to Massachusetts should nevertheless
not be unfavorably received in these new
colonies. He had, moreover, saved something
of his private fortune, though the family estates
were confiscated. His father, Sir William
Bouteler, had been killed at the battle of Cropredy Bridge two years before, and he, too, had
been seriously wounded at Naseby June 14,
1645, and for many days his life had been
despaired of. He described unto us the rout-
ing of the battle of Naseby, when even the
royal papers fell into the conqueror's hands, and
the final surrender at Bristol which took place
last September. Up to the new year he had
lain ill of his wounds, and recovering, had seen
Master Fenwick and had set sail from South-
hampton for Boston in March. He had had a
fair voyage, and landing in Boston and carrying
his letters to Governor Winthrop, had already
received a position in the commonwealth of
Massachusetts, and naught now remained but
for me to become his wife and return with him
to Boston, stopping for a brief space in Hartford, where he had been liberally entertained
by the Wolcotts and Master Sherman, who had
known my lady, and who desired greatly to
behold his bride, of whose beauty and favor he
said they were already fully assured.

"Oliver," said I, blushing for his saying this
before them all. "I am not prepared to marry

thee so quickly. It be a weighty matter to decide without thought. How can I marry without my father's consent and without telling Rosell? This I said weakly, for indeed I knew not what to say. But Oliver caught my hands and looked gravely down into my face.

"Little think we shall ever wed, fair Peace, if thou wait for thy father's consent, and that thou knowest full well? Thy father be chief friend to Cromwell, and thy sister Rosell was recently betrothed to one Master Ducksworth, a kinsman of Fairfax, one of the routers of Naseby, whom thou hast known in the past."

Then up spoke Dr. Peters and said that Master Fenwick had already spoken to him of the possibility of our marriage and that in these troublous times it were a great thing for a maid to have a true and faithful man for a protector, and that Mistress Mary already knew of the quest of young Sir Oliver and approved the marriage. That at any moment the settlement at Saybrooke might be left by them, for if Master Fenwick did not return in a few years he had given orders that his children should be taken to him.

"Doth thou desire this man for a husband, Mistress Peace?" he asked, as I still delayed my answer.

"Sometime," I said at last, faintly, "but I would like more time for courting."

"Nothing stands in the way of thy being

7

joined together save thy wayward will, young
mistress. Thy lady cousin desired it and thou
hath the consent of all present, and surely
through five years thou hast had time enough
for thinking." -

Then I turned and held out my hand to
Oliver and said:

"I will be thy wedded wife." And Dr. Peters
held our hands together for a moment and the
Mistresses Mary and Elizabeth kissed me, and
when I went up stairs to bed I heard them
planning together about my wedding clothes,
as if I had no part in the matter.

Two days later. This morning I arose and
looked out towards where the sun was rising
over the river, where only a few years since
Pequots and Narragansetts fought like savage
men. All was calm and peaceful, and as I
beheld the brown houses of our little settlement, I felt loath to leave it. I have to-day
taken from my chest the blue-figured dimity
and the white lute-string ribands which Rosell
sent me. Little did I think it would ever be
used for my wedding gown. Mistress Mary
hath been helping me to fashion it and hath
given me a kerchief of fine lawn and Mistress
Elizabeth a jewelled heart which belonged to
Lady Alice. Masters Mason and Huntington
hath also been here to-day to bid me joy, and

the news of my marriage hath spread among
all who dwelleth at Saybrooke. They be somewhat grave, for it be no matter for merriment
this bringing of the wilderness into captivity,
yet a wedding be a wedding the world over.
It hath the sound of fiddles in it and it be full
of right hearty love and good will.

❦❦

Yesterday we were married, and they said I
looked not unlike a bride in my dimity over
a white satin petticoat, and Oliver liked me
the better for the blue forget-me-nots on my
gown. As I was looking my last in the mirror
little Elizabeth brought me a bunch of daffodils
from the garden and I wore them, all unmind-
ful of poor Master Higginson and the four dead
daffodils that lay a year ago on the garden seat.
I need not Master Herrick's divinations now.
We were married in the garden under one of
John Winthrop's apple trees which had blossomed on purpose for my wedding day, and the
sun never shone and the birds never sung more
merrily than on the morning of May 10, 1646.
Afterwards we had a wedding feast and much
fun and laughter, and everyone said they would
miss me, and for a brief space Lady Peace
Bouteler were the most important woman in
the whole united colonies. Warwick came to
my wedding with a white cockade tied to his
neck and the rabbits were let out to make all

the havoc they could, and Baby Dorothy cooed like a wood pigeon, as she sat on Master Baldwin's coat on the grass, as Dr. Peters pronounced us man and wife. I am sure if we had been in old England we could not have had a merrier wedding. To-morrow we begin the long journey to Boston, going through Hartford, where Oliver's friends await us. Last night Oliver and I visited my lady's grave in the moonlight and I laid my wedding flowers in the shape of a star upon it and prayed I might be as good a wife as she had been. Afterwards we sat together on the garden seat and said pleasant things to each other, while the moon made a silver track across the water. Then it was that once again I saw my lady dressed all in white walk down the garden border and wave her hand in blessing and farewell ere she vanished in the silver moonlight on the sea. I had told my husband all about her, and though he could not see her as clearly as I could, he still thought he saw a shadowy figure standing on the waters' brink before it faded into silver light.

To-day we leave old Fort Point forever, though Oliver, my husband, saith "forever be a long time." Now that the parting hour hath come, such is the changeableness of woman, I am loath to depart. I love the river where it peacefully weds the sea. I love much of our life, and mostly do I hate to leave baby Dorothy, and the spot where my dear Lady Alice Fenwick sleeps until the resurrection morn. But my last hour here has come and I must end this little book that hath been the solace of so many weary hours. I wonder, a little timidly, of what lies beyond the vast forests to the northward where I must begin a larger book of life, but whatever the future may hold I and my true love, now united forever, shall meet it henceforth hand in hand. Thus little book, written not now for my impossible children, I sign my new name, token that all's well that ends well.

PEACE BOUTELER.

FORT POINT, SAYBROOKE, May 13, 1646.

Flavia ended the narrative and left a pensive group about the fire. She glanced over toward the corner where Richard and Phyllis sat behind the tea table and thought she saw their hands meet behind the tea cups, but it might not have been so, for they sat in deep shadow. The driftwood which Mark and Luke had brought in, in the early morning, had nearly burnt itself away, though Harry had been constantly in care of it and built the fire in economical fortresses, with Penelope to help him. He said it was because of her name, the Lady Penelope of unraveled webs, that when Flavia had finished the fire was smouldering and only occasionally bursting into flame. Maud had been sketching the four

men as they sat in the firelight. Carlotta
promptly lighted the parlor lamps and stole
from the room to beat up a Welch Rabbit and
for beer. Thus ends all romance in mundane
things. Harry went to the kitchen for more
wood and rebuilt the fire. The wind was blowing a regular Pequot-Narragansett War gale,
across the old north cove, and it suddenly came
upon them that it was their last night in the
old house. Others might come next summer as
Flavia's guests, but they might never come
again, and a little chill of sadness stole over
them, until Adel asked Flavia some question
about Peace Apsley's diary which loosened their
tongues. Whether the MS. was true or not,
they all believed in its authenticity, and were for
having it either made known to the public or
registered among colonial records. Mark was
very doubtful about the genuineness of the dog
rhyme to Master Higgins, and they were left in
doubt as to whether it were written by Mistress
Flavia of the 19th century, or Mistress Peace
of the 17th century.

"Just how much of that did you write your-
self?" asked Luke.

"I rewrote the whole of this diary. I had to
often supply words and sense, but I changed it
as little from the original document as possible,"
answered Flavia with dignity.

"The two Evangelists had better be careful
what they say," said Maud. "Luke ought to

be called 'doubtful Thomas'; he was mis-named." Phillis and Richard here became anxious to know what became of Peace Apsley and her husband after they had left Fort Point, and Flavia again grew suspicious of those shadowy hands behind the cups. The little party broke up when Carlotta announced supper in the dining-room, and an hour later the men sallied forth into the teeth of a northeast gale and returned to the little hotel at the Point, leaving the maidens to retire for their last night's sleep under the old roof tree which for several hundred years had sheltered so many sorrowful or joyful hearts.

"Dear old house," said Maud, as she went about with Flavia closing blinds and shutting down windows. "What a jolly, good time we have had in you! How many people have had a jolly, good time in you? Your walls should fairly crack with laughter, your beams jump up and down for joy. You should be called Merriment Cottage or Laughter Lodge!"

"Shades of the Puritans!" exclaimed Phillis sleepily from the other room. "Remember Maud, you belong to a sober commonwealth. You're not in Paris, just come back from the Opera Comique. It is past midnight. Put out the lights and go to bed."

🌱🌱

Next day they were all scattered, and the old

brown house by the roadside had entered into
its long winter rest. They persuaded Flavia
that her time could not be better employed than
in carefully editing the treasured MS., and in
investigating into the final destiny of each of
the inmates of the Fort in Peace Apsley's time,
as they all desired the narrative to end like an
old-fashioned play with all the characters on
the stage and blissfully or otherwise disposed
of.

Of the subsequent career of Colonel George
Fenwick, she found that in July, 1646, he was
appointed by Parliament one of the commissioners to establish and secure peace between
England and Scotland. In May, 1647, he was
serving the army in Ireland. The next year
he was in the north with his friend, Sir A. Haselrigge, Governor of New Castle, acting for the
Parliament. In 1648, he commanded Northumberland's newly raised regiment, and in July
he participated in a gallant victory against
Langdale's forces under Sir Richard Tempest,
for which a public thanksgiving was ordered by
Parliament. In October, 1651, he was appointed
one of the commissioners for the affairs of Scotland, a commission in which he was associated
with Chief Justice St. John, Sir Harry Vane,
General Monk, and other leaders of the parlia-
mentary party. Other records also say that he
was appointed, but did not act, as a judge in the
trial of Charles I, 1649, as he had also been for
many years a lawyer of Grey's Inn.

In 1652, he was made governor of Berwick, and in November of the same year he married at Clapham in Surray, for his second wife, Kathrene, daughter of Sir Arthur Haselrigge.

In 1656, Colonel Fenwick was returned as a member for Berwick in Cromwell's new Parliament, but he did not meet with the approbation of the council, Cromwell being now supreme. His last appearance in public life is as one of the subscribers to a remonstrance addressed to the Speaker of the House, September, 1656, inveighing against the unwarrantable usurpation of power and infringement of the liberties of Parliament by Cromwell.

He died in the ensuing spring, and his epitaph in the church at Berwick reads thus:

Col. George Fenwick,
of Brinkburn, Esq.
Governor of Berwick in the year
1652.

Was a principal instrument of causing this church to be built, and died March 15th, 1656.

A good man is a public good.

After Peace Apsley's departure from Saybrooke, the family lingered there only till the children were old enough to be carried to their father in England. The little Elizabeth married her cousin, Roger Fenwick of Stanton, while Baby Dorothy, the younger sister, married Sir Thomas Williamson of East Markham, in Nottinghamshire, and afterwards of North

4*

Wearmouth Hall, County of Durham. She died
Nov. 4, 1699, on her birthday, aged fifty-four.

Mistress Elizabeth Fenwick, Colonel Fenwick's sister, married May 20, 1648, Captain
John Cullick, a prominent citizen of Hartford
from 1648 to 1658. He removed with his wife
to Boston in 1659, where doubtless his wife once
more met Peace Bouteler. He died there in
January, 1663, and the Mistress Elizabeth made
another venture on the matrimonial sea and
married Richard Ely of Boston. She had a son,
John Cullick, by her first husband, whò gradu-
ated at Harvard College in 1668, and two
daughters, Elizabeth and Mary. Elizabeth
married Benjamin Batten of Boston, and he it
was who erected the monument to the memory
of Lady Fenwick as it now stands, as appears
by the receipt of Matthew Griswold, given in
1659, and recorded in Saybrook.

Of Mistress Mary Fenwick, Flavia could find
no record, save that the winter after Peace Apsley's departure from Fort Point, there was
found an uncertain record of the death of one
of Colonel Fenwick's relatives, which, as nought
further could be found of Mistress Mary, might
have been that lady.

Of good Master Higginson the accounts were
brief, save that after serving with Rev. Henry
Whitfield at Guilford, he was called to minister
to the church in Salem, where he remained a
faithful minister of God's Word until he was
called to the Heavenly Salem beyond.

In 1647 the first fort within the enclosure of which Lady Fenwick was buried was destroyed by fire, and in the following year the new fort was built close to the river's brink, the earthworks of which are within the memory of many still living, as it was not destroyed till 1870.

❦❦

Flavia looked in vain for further records of Peace Apsley, but found out absolutely nothing, and had almost given it up in despair until one day she was invited out to dinner in Boston by some friends whom she had met while traveling in England, but whom she had never visited before. She found them living in a charming house, and dinner was served in a delightful oak wainscoted dining-room, hung with family portraits. Flavia, who sat opposite the fireplace, was especially attracted by the portrait of a very beautiful young woman, in a filmy dress of blue and white, with a single brilliant on a piece of dark velvet round her throat. Her head was set against a background of apple boughs, and she wore daffodils on her breast and in her hair. Flavia became more and more attracted by the charming face, full of wit and brilliance. The brown hair was brushed up from the forehead and fell in little rebellious curls about the delicate pink shells of ears, while the blue eyes seem to gleam with secret laughter. Presently the conversation fell on family portraits, and their host discoursed fluently on Copley, Gainsborough, and Stuart, while he made his wife nervous by wiping his fingers vigorously on the priceless doylie under his finger bowl, a habit some men have. What he was saying, however, was far more interesting to Flavia than all the lace doylies in Christendom, for he gave her opportunity of asking about the portrait opposite her. Then Madame, her hostess, flushed with honest pride and forgot all about the crushed doylie.

"That is a portrait," she said, "of my ancestress, Lady Peace Bouteler, who was a great beauty and leader of society here in early colonial days, but who returned to England after the Restoration. Let me see, I think she had some connection with your early Connecticut history, for she came out with the Fenwicks and settled at Saybrook in — well, some time in the 17th century. I have so much to do I can never remember dates."

"Was her maiden name Peace Apsley?" asked Flavia.

"Yes. What a memory you have for history! I did not know she was prominent enough to have found her way into the colonial records."

Flavia smiled and dipped her finger-tips into the rose-colored finger-bowl contentedly. After dinner she went and stood for a long time in front of the fireplace, looking into the face of Peace Apsley, painted in her wedding gown. The happy smile, the delicate hands told the story of peace and plenty. Flavia closed her eyes for a moment and summoned back the vision of that old colonial life, until she could almost smell apple blossoms and pick daffodils. She thought also of the dear house party and their last night in the old house. Of Richard and Phillis, now married; of Harry and Penelope, engaged; of Helen and Maud, back in Paris, leading the old artist life, and of one of their company who had gone a long journey to the better land. Then she opened her eyes again and found Peace Apsley looking down into her face, with the same frank smile, and it seemed as if she were meeting some dear old friend once more, and as if no time had passed since the portrait was painted, long ago.

"You seem fascinated with my ancestress," said her hostess beside her.

"I am," said Flavia. "Tell me more about her? Did she go back to England and what was her subsequent life?"

Her hostess laughed. "I am so sorry I cannot tell you; you see it all happened so long ago, and to tell you the truth the present is so much more interesting, and I am so much interested in diet-kitchens and education and Buddhism."

And with that Flavia had to be content, and she was, for she always felt after that as if she had seen a vision of Peace just as Peace Apsley herself once saw the white vision of Lady Fenwick come down the garden path at Fort Point.

❧❧

Things have changed now down at the old harbor town. Thirty-five years have perhaps wrought more changes than in all the centuries before. The fort has gone, not a vestige of it remains. Huge iron birds, full of blackness and smoke and moulten fire, with death in their path fly on steel rails across where once the old colonial life was lived, across the garden where Peace Apsley used to sit and where the Lady Alice once stood looking wistfully across the blue waters. Lady Fenwick now rests with many others in the old graveyard at the Point, who have served the state and commonwealth in past days. Her grave, which was a lonely landmark for so many years, ceased to be so when she was reinterred in 1870, with appropriate commemorative services. Sometimes in crossing the fields near where she rested you may yet pick bits of lavender and wonder whether they are estrays from her herb garden. Across the field and on the edge of the marsh you may see late in August a gorgeous hedge of rose mallows and wonder whether she found strange merits in mallows for the sick. The whistle of the engine, the noise of nineteenth century civilization, long since drove away her walking spirit. Probably Peace Bouteler saw her apparition for the last time in the moonlight in the garden on the evening of her wedding day. Call it, however, a ghostly presence or a pervading influence, or what you like, her presence still does linger over this land of her adoption. It comes to us as the sweet melody of a half forgotten tune or as a nosegay of old memories 'mid the rush of nineteenth century life. There is very little of the real about it, but that little is fragrant and filled with the heroic devotion to duty, strong fibre of character and the high courage of those women of the old time life who were among our pioneer settlers. As we stand beside her tomb in the old graveyard at Saybrook Point, we may gain a mental vision at least of stately beauty and of gentle culture, and feel our hearts thrill with a finer courage and a more exalted sense of life and its purpose, through the memory of this lady of the olden time.